NUSH

MR BOLTON

SIOBHAN
BRANAGAN

AMELIA
DE LA COURT

MR MEETON

MS
BIRKINSTEAD

MAL

DUNCAN
CLIFFHEAD

ORC

THE BEARD BROTHERS

VIKING

WIL

KINS WEL

KIN

CORNER BOY
GILLIGAN

Rory Branagan (Detective)
The Deadly Dinner Lady

by Andrew Clover
and Ralph Lazar

DANGER

RORY BRANAGAN
(DETECTIVE)

MS RHODES

CASSIDY
CALLAGHAN

SEAMUS
BRANAGAN

STEPHEN MAYSMITH

MRS WELKIN

MS DINEFIELD

NIGEL
BINAISA

MRS WINSCOMBE

MARY
SEACOLE

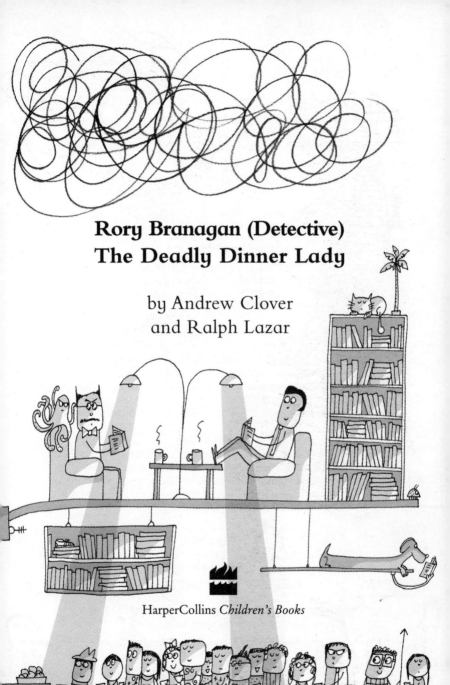

Rory Branagan (Detective)
The Deadly Dinner Lady

by Andrew Clover
and Ralph Lazar

HarperCollins *Children's Books*

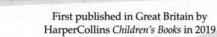

First published in Great Britain by
HarperCollins *Children's Books* in 2019
HarperCollins *Children's Book*s is a division of HarperCollins*Publishers* Ltd,
HarperCollins Publishers
1 London Bridge Street
London SE1 9GF

The HarperCollins website address is
www.harpercollins.co.uk

3

Text copyright © Andrew Clover 2019
Illustrations copyright © Ralph Lazar 2019
Cover design copyright © HarperCollins*Publishers* Ltd 2019
All rights reserved.

ISBN 978–0–00–826592–2

Andrew Clover and Ralph Lazar assert the moral right to be identified as
the author and illustrator of the work respectively.
A CIP catalogue record for this title is available from the British Library.

Printed and bound in England by CPI Group (UK) Ltd, Croydon, CR0 4YY

MIX
Paper from
responsible sources
FSC™ C007454
FSC
www.fsc.org

This book is produced from independently certified FSC™ paper
to ensure responsible forest management.

For more information visit: www.harpercollins.co.uk/green

We dedicate this story to all teachers who go that extra mile to make their lessons interesting – and to the kids who listen to them.

There comes a time in every schoolchild's day when we must leave the *protection* of the teachers . . .

. . . and go into the *lair* of the Dinner Ladies.

The Dinner Hall is always HOT and NOISY. Smoke *drifts* from the kitchen. And there, snarling like *DRAGONS*, lurk the *Dinner Ladies*.

'QUIET!' they *roar* as they *bang* their trays with their spoons.

Our Head Dinner Lady is called Ms Rhodes, but we call her *the Toad*. Her eyes BULGE as she *splats* down your mince.

The next is called Mrs Winscombe. No one has ever heard her speak.

And the third is Ms Dinefield – the most *gorgeous* dinner lady in the world.

'Would you like peach crumble?' she says.

'Yes!'

'Custard?'

'YES!'

Everyone *LOVES* peach crumble. I swear . . .

When I am older, I sometimes think I'll be a *detective*, and have a high-up tree house with special swings so I can SWOOP down (when I see a crime).

But *other* times I think . . .

I'll have a *big castle made from crumble,*
and I'll spend my days eating the walls.

We all LOVE peach crumble. Everyone tries to get more.

Even Mr Bolton (our deputy head). He stands behind Ms Dinefield *ogling* it with his beady eyes. He doesn't even *notice* if you try to steal a yoghurt.

I think he likes Ms Dinefield too.

But I reckon *she* likes Mr Meeton. He is the *coolest* teacher by a million miles. He has cool hair, and cool shoes.

He's a LEGEND.

He's got a blog called *SuperMeet*.
Literally *each* time you go on there
Mr Meeton will be *hang-gliding*...

or canoeing over Niagara Falls ...

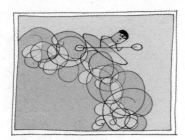

or hanging with some pop stars, telling a joke.

Mr Meeton does not even CARE if you take a yoghurt.

But the Toad does. You put ONE FINGER on her yoghurts, and suddenly she'll LEAP OUT.

'*Don't TOUCH my YOGHURTS,*' she'll *croak*, and as she *grabs* them she'll *jab* you with her spoon.

EVERYONE **hates her.** (I'm so sorry to say it, but they do.)

But WHO would actually try to KILL *her?*

And **WHY?**

And *HOW?*

Because *that's* what happens.

I have to investigate.

I end up *SNEAKING* round the whole school, knowing that at each turn there could be the *very deadliest of deadly dangers*. There could even be A KILLER.

I'll tell you the whole story.

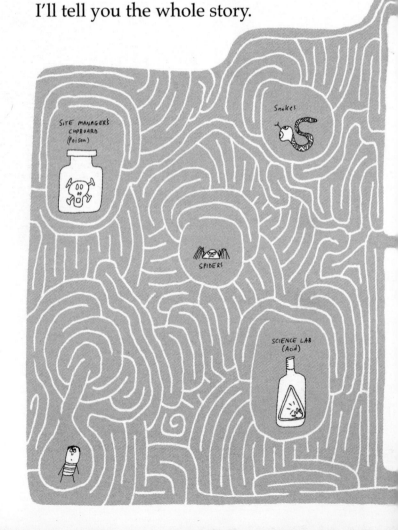

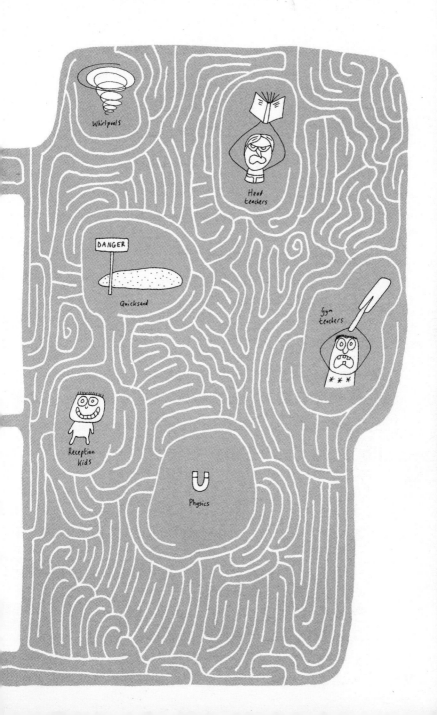

CHAPTER ONE:
Brilliant

It all starts on a bright Monday morning. I am actually in a good mood (even though I'm going to school).

It is only one week since I solved the Big Cash Robbery. As I come out of my house, my friend Corner Boy sees me and he sings, '*RORY BRANAGAN! (He's a detective!) RORY BRANAGAN! (He'll solve all your crimes!)*'

Which I like. We're being watched by some kids from Year Two.

'Why are you singing that?' asks one.

Corner Boy tells him the whole story.

'Is it true?' the kid asks me.

'It is,' I tell him. 'I ended up climbing into the house of Ms Turkey-head *the head teacher*! We thought *she*'d taken the money!'

I am now acting it all out. I leap up on to a garden wall.

'I had to climb along a deadly *high* ledge to reach a window,' I say.

'If I'd fallen from there,' I tell my fans, 'I would have been *crushed like a grape*!!'

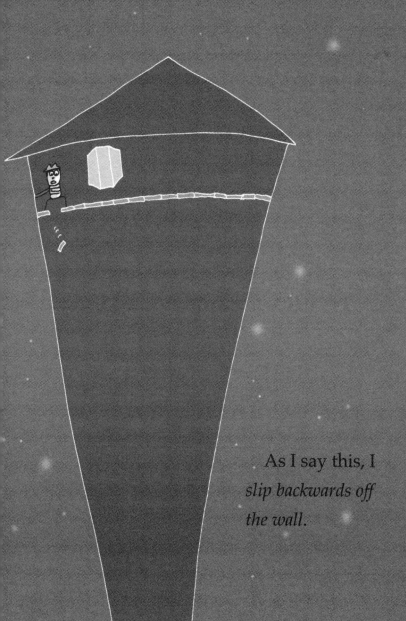

As I say this, I
*slip backwards off
the wall.*

I end up by a couple of gnomes.
One gives me a bad bruise with his
wheelbarrow. The other looks like he's
about to GET me with his fishing rod.

As I climb back on to the wall to escape
the evil gnomes, I find . . .

My Best Friend and Accomplice, *Cassidy Callaghan*, giving me a cool, catty look.

'One of these days your big mouth will get you into Big Trouble,' she says.

I am so pleased to see her.

'Trouble,' I tell her, 'is *my* middle name.'

'No,' she says. 'Your middle name is *Dougal*.'

'My name is Rory Dougal *Trouble* Branagan,' I tell her. 'And *I blow my nose* at Trouble, and I *slap my bottom at Danger*.'

I slap my bottom now. *Everyone* laughs.
I jump down off the wall, and we all set off together.

We are all in *brilliant* moods all the way to school – where we hear a *surprise*.

'This term,' Mr Bolton announces in School Assembly, 'we will be holding *St Bart's Got Talent*, in which YOU will be invited to *sing*, *dance* or *perform*. And I, my friends, have prepared a RAP.'

Already, everyone is trying not to *laugh*.
'Mr Bolton,' asks Corner Boy, '*what* will
your rap be about?'

'I shall be rapping about *grammar*,' says Mr Bolton. 'Specifically . . . about *Incorrect Uses of the Apostrophe*.' And he holds up an apostrophe, as if he's holding up a BOMB.

CHAPTER TWO:
The Talent

One week later, we have the first round of the talent show. It's not like a *real* talent show – on live TV, on Saturday night. It's after lunch, on a Tuesday, in the Dinner Hall. The host is Ms Turkey-head.

And the first act is Corner Boy.

He sings '*Rory Branagan! (He's a Detective!)*', with Duncan Cliffhead on drums and Nigel Binaisa on French horn.

Even though the song's about me, I have to say . . . it's TERRIBLE. But at least it only lasts ten seconds.

Up next is Amelia de la Court, a very dramatic girl in my year. *She* tries to sing the whole album *21* by Adele.

Ms Turkey-head has to cut her off.

I have an important job in the show myself. I am in charge of *Backstage Security*.

I escort Amelia off to the *Backstage Area* (actually the kitchen).

And next up is Mr Bolton.

It turns out Mr Bolton hasn't just
prepared a rap, he's also prepared SIGNS,
and he waves those signs as he goes . . .

'CATS *means* LOTS OF CATS.

CAT'S *means* BELONGING TO THE
CAT . . .'

We can't *believe* it. The rap is definitely STUPID, but it is CATCHY, and Mr Bolton is performing it surprisingly WELL.

'*These are the rules of apostrophes,*' he goes. '*There are two exceptions – learn them, please!*'

Now a backing track starts going *BOOM BOOM BOOM BOOM*, and Mr Bolton starts BOUNCING as he goes . . .

'IT'S is short for IT IS.
ITS means BELONGING TO IT.

WHO'S is short for WHO IS.
WHOSE means BELONGING TO
WHO.'

He finishes: *'These are the rules of apostrophes. If you forget them, kiss my SHOE.'*

And then Mr Bolton does a gangsta-style pointing-to-the-shoe move. He freezes.

One second later, we all . . .

BURST INTO APPLAUSE.

It's not often we get the chance to *delay afternoon school for as long as possible,* just by *cheering* for Mr Bolton . . . The crowd takes that chance.

Everyone is cheering.

They *surge* to the front of the stage.
They invite Mr Bolton to *crowd-surf*.

Which he does.

Mr Bolton actually ENJOYS himself.
Till they drop him.

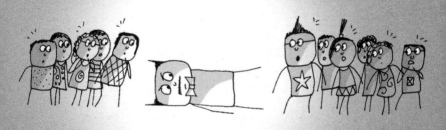

Everyone's still cheering as I lead him
away.

CHAPTER THREE:
Even More Deadly

I escort Mr Bolton into the Backstage Area.
The Dinner Ladies now give him a cheer.

'Well done,' says the Toad. 'You
knocked 'em DEAD!'

'That was *AMAZING*!' says Ms
Dinefield. 'Don't you think so, Mr
Meeton?'

Mr Meeton is there too. He's tuning his guitar, with his foot up on some peas.

'It was good,' he says. 'I actually filmed it and posted it on *SuperMeet*. But most MCs rap about *girls* or *guns* – not *grammar*.'

'I don't care,' says Mr Bolton. 'If I can STAMP OUT all *bad apostrophes* from this school it'll be worth it.'

'What do you make of this one?' asks Mr Meeton.

He points to a whiteboard where the Toad has written that today's lunch will be . . . 'sausage with mash and pea's'.

As Mr Bolton looks at that word, *Pea's*, he goes all *still* as if he's covered in deadly bees. It's actually *funny*.

Mr Meeton is still smiling as he *swaggers* out for his song. He puts his foot up on the amp and he ROCKS OUT to 'Stairway to Heaven' by Led Zep.

He is . . . *incredibly* good. But he's not as funny as Mr Bolton. At the end he tries to crowd-surf, but no one's ready. He sort of... *flops* off the stage.

Ms Turkey-head is already announcing the next act. 'Up next it's Ms Rhodes – the *deadly* Dinner Lady!'

And the Toad LEAPS out. *'Rebbit!'* she says (croaking like a toad). No one's *expecting* that. We all ROAR with laughter.

The Toad then does an impression of Duncan Cliffhead doing the drums. *Bang, bang, bang.* Then she does an imitation of Amelia.

Then she puts her foot up, and she pretends to ROCK OUT like Mr Meeton, except with a Turkey Twizzler.

No one knew the Toad was funny! *Everyone* laughs.

Mr Meeton is the only one who doesn't. I'm watching him as he heads out the back of the Dinner Hall.

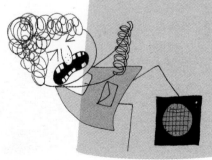

Most people are watching the stage.

'Have you got anything else for us, Ms Rhodes?' Ms Turkey-head asks.

'I do!' says the Toad. *'And it's a yoghurt!'* she says, whipping one out.

Ms Turkey-head is JUST about to touch it.

'Don't touch my yoghurt!' says the Toad. She snatches it away and walks off.

Now . . . this is probably not the funniest joke that's ever happened in the world. But it's definitely the funniest one *in our school*. You could probably hear the laugh from SPACE.

HA HA HA HA HA HA HA HA HA HA HA HA HA HA HA HA HA HA HA HA HA HA HA HA HA HA HA HA HA HA HA HA HA HA HA HA HA HA HA HA HA HA HA HA HA HA HA HA HA HA HA HA HA HA HA HA HA HA HA HA HA HA HA HA HA HA HA HA HA HA HA HA HA HA HA HA HA HA HA HA HA

Next up are Nush and Mal, who do a Beyoncé song. Everyone loves that too. We're all so hyped now.

Suddenly Cat Callaghan comes *slinking* in from the back of the Dinner Hall, wearing a hat.

'Where have you been?' I ask.

'I just nipped up to the Drama Studio,' she says. 'And I nicked this hat.'

This bothers me.

'We are detectives,' I tell her. 'I can't let you *steal* a hat.'

'The door was *open*,' she says. '*Anyone* could have stolen one!'

'Anyone *could*. *You* did!'

'I shut the door after me,' she says. 'I also shut the door to the flat roof – that was open too. I probably *prevented* more crimes!'

I want to say more, but Ms Turkey-head is announcing Cat from the stage.

'The last act is Cassidy Callaghan,' she says.

'Rory,' Cat whispers, 'lift my foot and FLING me.'

And I do. And that's how . . .

The Cat takes the stage by doing a
backflip that's two metres high.

She's a cat. She lands *perfectly*.

She hits her position.

Then to loud music she does an
EXPLOSION of leaps and backflips and
weird *catlike CARTWHEELS*.

At the end, *everyone* is cheering.

'Right,' says Ms Turkey-head, 'we will now call back onstage all the acts who've performed. And we will select three acts for the final based on who gets the biggest cheer.'

She turns to me in the wings.

'Rory,' she says, 'we need everyone from backstage. Would you mind calling them?'

I don't mind at all.

I open the door to the Backstage Area.
Cat comes with me. I am a detective
so as I go into that room I NOTICE
EVERYTHING.

Mrs Winscombe, chopping food

Nigel Binaisa, polishing his French horn

Nush and Mal, doing hair

'All acts must go back onstage,' I announce.

And I'm almost *crushed* as Amelia comes stampeding by.

Duncan Cliffhead, looking for crumble

Mr Bolton, listening to Amelia's story about her X Factor audition

'Where are Corner Boy and Ms Rhodes?' I ask.

'She went out the back door,' says Ms Dinefield.

Mrs Winscombe goes out to get her.

I wait for her to reappear.

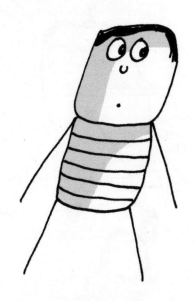

But she doesn't. Suddenly I get a *very bad feeling*. Then . . .

A SCREAM *RIPS* THROUGH
THE AIR.

AHHHHHHHHHHHH'!

You can tell something HORRIBLE has happened.

Right away, BIG DETECTIVE
THOUGHTS *shoot* through my head like
rockets.

I'm thinking . . .

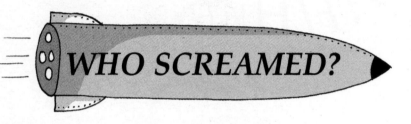

I'm thinking . . .

I'm thinking . . .
This sounds like a case for Cat and Deadly!

Mrs Winscombe appears at the back door. She's white.

'Quick!' she says. 'It's Ms Rhodes!'

We both RUN.

We leap through the door.

We find ourselves in a small yard I've never seen before. On one side it has the tall back walls of the old factory. On the other there's the even higher back wall of the school. In front of that there's a bin.

Ms Rhodes is lying on the ground. She
has a rectangular bruise on her head. I
only look at her for half a second.
But I'm pretty sure she's DEAD.

Mr Bolton appears.

He looks at Ms Rhodes. He looks at us.

'The whole school will collect,' he tells me, 'in FIRE ASSEMBLY POSITIONS. Right NOWWWW!'

EMERGENCY EXIT

CHAPTER FOUR:
The First Interviews of the Case

And, five minutes later, the whole school *is* outside in Fire Assembly Positions. But they're not taking it well.

'Oh my God,' Amelia de la Court is saying, 'it is *freezing*!'

I think: *She was one of the SUSPECTS who was in that kitchen.* I approach.

'I don't know WHY we're outside!' she says.

'It is because the dinner lady *has just been killed*!' I tell her, and I look *furiously* into her eyes for her reaction.

'Well, I'm not *surprised*,' she says. 'Some of the food they serve is DISGUSTING.'

I can't *believe* she would say this now.
I'm also OFFENDED.

'You *cannot* say that,' I tell her, 'about
the peach crumble!'

'The crumble's all DRY,' she says, 'and
the custard's always LUMPY.'

'Then you should have yoghurt,' I tell
her. 'Or the Fruit Option.'

'I'm not having the Fruit Option,' she spits. 'Those apples are always *brown*, and the bananas are all *squidgy*. I've told the Toad a *million* times, and she just won't listen!'

'Is that why you killed her?' I ask.

She says, *'What?'*

'Is that why you KILLED her?' I ask again.

But she doesn't answer. She just staggers back to Nush and Mal, and she *faints*.

'What happened?' asks Corner Boy, who has just appeared.

'Rory's just killed Amelia,' says Duncan Cliffhead.

'I haven't *killed* her!' I say. 'She's only *fainted*. I'm not even sure she's fainted – she's probably putting it on!'

'I am NOT putting it on!' says Amelia (waking up). 'You just asked a HORRIBLE QUESTION, and I *fainted*—'

'And you still haven't answered it,' I say. *'Did you kill Ms Rhodes?'*

She doesn't answer. She just faints again.

'Look,' says Nush, 'Amelia was in the kitchen the whole time, telling a long story to Mr Bolton. She *couldn't* have done it!'

'I would suspect the people who *disappeared* from that kitchen,' says Mal.

'Who did that?' I ask.

'Corner Boy, for one,' she replies.

And now my blood runs cold.

A FEW FACTS ABOUT CORNER BOY:

1. He sometimes carries a spear. And . . .

2. If you so much as TOUCH his
   glasses, he goes BERSERK.

I actually *like* him. But if I had to put my
money on one person who might LOSE IT
and start *lashing out* at dinner ladies, it'd
be him.

I approach him.

'Corner Boy,' I ask, *'where were you when the crime was committed?'*

It's the question detectives have been asking since the beginning of crime. And I get a reply they've *never* received.

'I was doing a poo,' says Corner Boy.

'You were about to go back onstage,' I tell him. 'Why would you—'

'And I could FEEL the poo COMING OUT,' says Corner Boy (very loudly). 'It was a BIG one, and . . .'

Suddenly I have the *panicky* feeling that Corner Boy is about to give me WAY TOO MUCH INFORMATION about his poo. I know what he's like. In no time his poo will be like a PERSONAL FRIEND who might start saying 'Hello' in the playground.

My mum will be inviting it round on sleepovers.

'Corner Boy,' I shout, 'you are giving me TOO MUCH INFORMATION! *I can't take it!*'

'Then you will NEVER be a detective,' says Corner Boy. '*And I will solve this crime before you do!*'

Now THAT just annoys me. I am about to tell him to SHUT UP.

But just then Ms Turkey-head appears.

'I regret to say that the school will be closed for a POLICE INVESTIGATION,' she announces. 'Your parents will be here shortly.'

CHAPTER FIVE:
Detective *Frenzy*

But *my* mum does NOT come *at all*.

I don't really mind, though. I turn, and I am very happy to see . . .

My neighbour Mrs Welkin, standing there with my good friend Wilkins the sausage-dog detective.

As I go home, I tell Mrs Welkin
EVERYTHING.

'Someone HIT Ms Rhodes very hard on
the head,' I tell her. 'WHO would do that?'

'It's obvious,' says Mrs Welkin. 'It was
Mrs Winscombe.'

'But why would she do that?'

'Ms Rhodes has pushed Mrs Winscombe around for thirty-eight years,' says Mrs Welkin. 'You can only take a thing like that for so long – then you SNAP.'

This doesn't seem likely. I think Mrs Welkin is LEAPING to conclusions.

Suddenly it feels like that's what EVERYONE is doing.

Corner Boy is up ahead with his dad.

'RORY!' he shouts. 'Apparently
MS DINEFIELD killed Ms Rhodes!
Dad has been listening to the POLICE
RADIO. The police are *watching* the BUS
STATION, the TRAIN STATION and ALL
KNOWN CITY EXITS!'

I don't even know what *ALL KNOWN CITY EXITS* are!

I am trying to imagine, when . . .

Michael and Rupert ride towards us on bikes.

'*Corner Boy!*' they shout. 'We need as many people as possible! We're going to GET HER!'

'*I'll get my spear!*' says Corner Boy.

'But WHO are you getting?' I call as they go by.

'*Ms Turkey-head!*' they shout.

I am thinking: *People should NOT be CHASING head teachers through the woods with spears!*

It does not seem professional.

I am *very* bothered by all this. By now
Mrs Welkin and I have reached my house.

'I can't come in,' she says, 'but
apparently your BROTHER is here.'

I open my front door.

And right away, my brother's BIG
HEAD is there.

'Did you hear about the dinner lady?'
he says. '*I'm sure Mr Meeton did it!*'

That just *annoys* me. I know he's only saying this because he knows I like Mr Meeton.

'That is about the only person it could NOT have been,' I tell him. 'I saw Mr Meeton leave the Dinner Hall.'

'You just don't *want* it to have been him,' he says. 'You can't work out if you are *IN LOVE* with him, or if you *wish he was your dad*!'

As he says this, I can think of ONE MILLION REASONS why what he said was WRONG. (They're blasting in my head like firecrackers.) But there's *no point* talking to big brothers. They won't *listen*. So I don't *try* to explain.

I just . . . do a FLYING JUMP KICK at his head. I am not really trying to GET him. I fly over him *like a jet*.

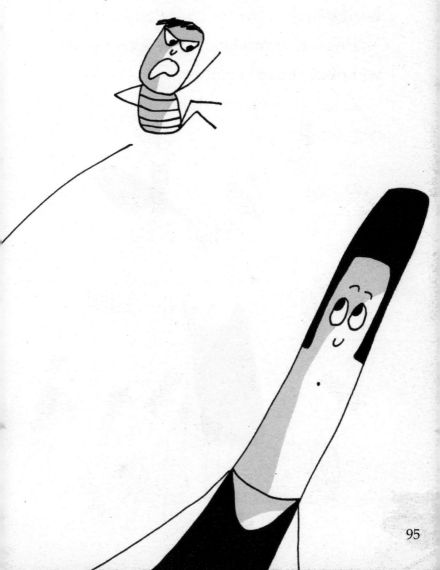

But it ends up with him sitting on me like I'm a chair.

'GET OFF ME!' I shout (wriggling).

'I won't,' he replies. 'I can tell you still want to get me.'

So then I freeze. At the same time I can't help but smile.

'And *now* I won't get off,' he says, 'because I can TELL you've just decided to *put something in my bed*.' And he does an EVIL SMILE . . .

As if he thinks he is a DETECTIVE GENIUS to know that, but he's NOT. I *always* put things in his bed when I'm annoyed with him. Last time it was a wet *flannel*. The time before it was a *worm*. That's what I do.

I think . . . if the president of China was annoyed with the president of Russia, who was annoyed with the president of the United States, they shouldn't have *long, long talks* in some *boring palace* somewhere.

They should just SNEAK into each
other's rooms and *leave things in their beds*
– something GOOD, like a *snail*, a *dead frog*
or even just a *sock*.

That is the world I dream of. I am
dreaming of it now.

My brother climbs off me, but he still wants to be mean.

'Mr Meeton has definitely *disappeared*,' he sneers.

'HOW DO YOU EVEN *KNOW* THAT?'

He gets out Mum's iPad, clicks on *SuperMeet* and shows me a picture of Mr Meeton playing guitar against a big sky.

'That was his last picture!' he says. 'He hasn't posted since two twenty-six.'

'*SO?*'

'He does his THOUGHT OF THE DAY at two forty-five. He does The Big Beverage at three fifteen. If *absolutely anything* happens at all, the man discusses it. He would definitely MENTION it if there was a MURDER. But he HASN'T. And I'm telling you:
he's GONE and he
AIN'T
COMING
BACK!'

'Well, I am sure there is some EXPLANATION *for that . . .*' I *start* to say, but I get a BIG LUMP in my throat, and I realise I am in *big DANGER* of crying.

I say nothing.

I run to my room. And only now do I CRY.

CHAPTER SIX:
Down a Deep, Dark Hole

I feel as if I am down in a deep, dark dungeon.

I'm thinking: *I am not IN LOVE with Mr Meeton! (That was such a MEAN thing to say!) But I definitely LIKE him.*

He has been about the only person who's been nice to me since Dad went!

And I do NOT wish he was my dad.

But I do sometimes forget what Dad
looks like and I know it was a bit like Mr
Meeton, so I do get them mixed up.

I cry more. *This*
is what happens to
everything I like.
I lose it.

I've *properly* cried now. If I *had* been down in a deep, dark dungeon, I would've *flooded* it with my tears by now and climbed out. I am actually *embarrassed* that I cried like that.

I stop. And just then I hear a *bang* behind me. I wipe my eyes. I turn.

I see Cat.

'You OK?' she says.

'*Yes!*' I tell her.

She then asks a question that brings me right to my senses.

'So who do you think killed Ms Rhodes?' she asks.

'I don't know,' I reply, 'but my HUNCH is Mr Bolton.'

Cat climbs through the window.
'How do you work that out?' she asks.

I tell her about how Mr Bolton saw the word *'pea's'* and went all still.

She smiles.

'Rory,' she says, 'are you *honestly* saying you imagine Mr Bolton might have killed her over *grammar*?'

I try to imagine it.

In my head Mr Bolton is saying,
'PEAS is a PLURAL so it does NOT take an apostrophe!'

And the Toad is saying, *'I'm SORRY, Mr Bolton!'*

'Sorry is NOT good enough,' He is saying, and he's chasing her out into the yard . . .

'I can definitely IMAGINE it,' I say.

'Well, it's a good theory,' she says. 'But Nush said Mr Bolton was in the kitchen, hearing a long story from Amelia de la Court.'

I suddenly remember that, and I realise I am actually A VERY BAD DETECTIVE. I'm *annoyed*. I'm also CONFUSED.

'But then we have no other real *suspects*,' I tell her, 'because you can only reach that yard through the kitchen, and it seems like no one went out that back door!'

Cat smiles. 'Rory Branagan,' she says, 'can YOU honestly not imagine *any* other way that killers *might* have got into that yard?'

I am thinking: *Well, they might have been rival dinner ladies who flew over the wall on dragons, ready to fight with saucepans and spoons . . .*

I'm thinking: *It might have been a whole army of garden gnomes, who came over the walls in a swarm...*

I can think of LOADS of ways they MIGHT have come in. But none seems very *likely*.

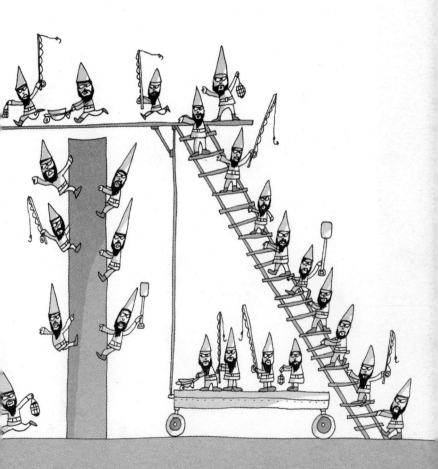

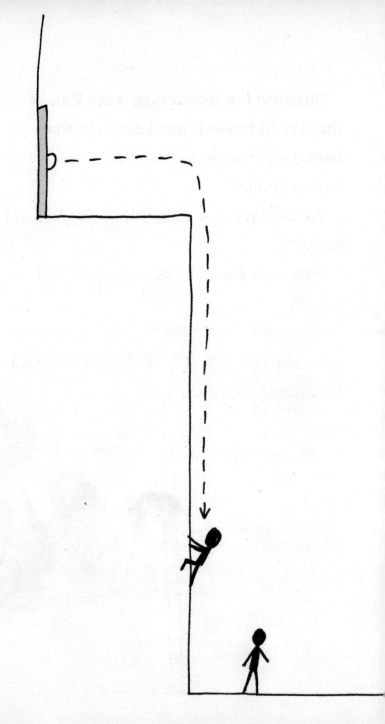

'Because *I'm* wondering,' says Cat, 'if they could have climbed down to that back yard *from the flat roof that's outside the Drama Studio!*'

As she says this, I am thinking: *She could be right!*

'*Where we know the door was OPEN,*' I say.

'*Because I closed it when I was up there later,*' she says. 'Well . . . I THINK that roof looks over the yard!'

'Cat!' I say. *'Will we go and look?'*

'Can I be honest?' she says.

'What?'

'I said I'd help you be a detective to find your dad – *not* to get in trouble with the police. And we've done that *three times*. My dad's told me to stop.'

'HAS he?' I say.

I've only ever seen her dad watching TV. I've never even heard him *speak*. I am actually *interested* in this.

But right now, I am ONE HECK OF A LOT MORE *INTERESTED* in the crime.

I also realise that there will be *real-life detectives* at school and they will be taking *photos* and *fingerprints* and

doing *very interesting detective things* –
and I am very, very *CURIOUS* to see
them.

I get my hat. I get my coat. And I go.

CHAPTER SEVEN:
Solo Investigations

I was wanting to see policemen, and I'm NOT disappointed. Five minutes later, I am at the school . . .

There are *loads* of them – all packed round the front of the building.

As I scoot round the side, I *think* I can see the roof outside the Drama Studio. I think there's a drainpipe coming down to that yard. But I can't see it to be sure.

I go round to the Old Factory. I climb
a tree that's growing by the wall. It is
BRILLIANT. I can see right into the yard.

I can see the
drainpipe. It's *broken*.
It stops about two
metres above the
ground.

I can see a bin. I can
also see a BIN-shaped
dry patch. It rained
today: I can see that
bin was MOVED.
Why?

I can see *glass*
glinting. I'm thinking:
What made that? I
can see ALL this.

Unfortunately . . .

I can *also* see . . . Stephen Maysmith, the police detective.

He comes out of the kitchen. Straight away, he sees *me*. It's not hard. I am right by the wall, clinging to the tree like a Christmas-tree Fairy.

'*YOU!*' he shouts. '*Climb down from that tree. Stay there. I will take you STRAIGHT HOME!*'

So then I figure: *I've learned all I can here.*

I climb down.

But then I think: *But he isn't here yet. I may as well go back round to the front of the school to SEE if I can get in.*

I rush back to the front.

I try to work out if *there's a way past them.*

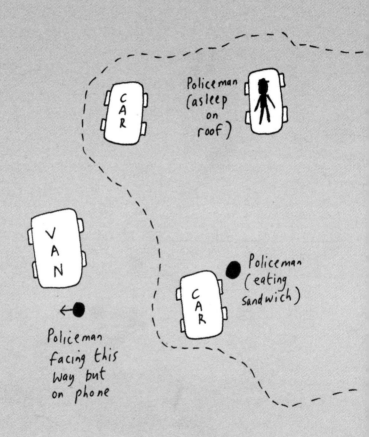

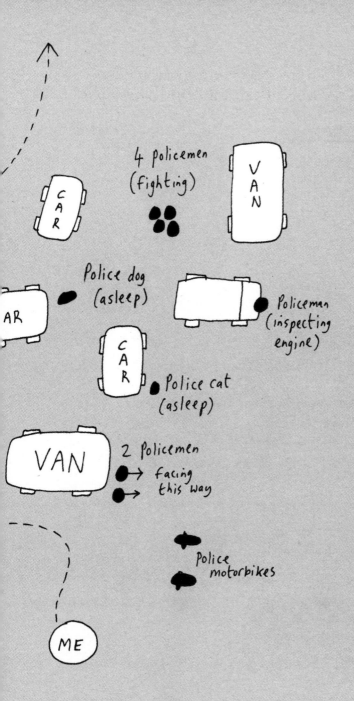

4 policemen
(fighting)

CAR

VAN

Police dog
(asleep)

AR

Policeman
(inspecting
engine)

CAR

Police cat
(asleep)

VAN

2 Policemen
facing
this way

Police
motorbikes

ME

Door
into
school

And I've noticed this:
if you act suspiciously,
people SUSPECT you.
But if you stay cool,
they don't notice you.
I flick past two first
policemen, cool as ice
cream.

POLICE

POLICE

But then I see Stephen Maysmith
hurrying over.

'*Young man!*' he shouts. '*Just WHAT do
you think you are doing?*'

I don't want to answer that. I just
SPRINT.

But he is on me like a big spacehopper.
BOING.

'Stop right there!' he says.
'I need to go in!' I tell him.
'But WHY?'
'I need my PE kit!'
'You do NOT need your PE kit!'
'I DO! Or my socks will get STINKY!'

He doesn't know WHAT to say to that.
He's BAMBOOZLED.

I quickly ask *him* questions.

'Have you found Mr Meeton?' I ask.

'No!' he says.

'So you ARE looking for him?'

'ENOUGH! *I cannot disclose Police Business!*' he says.

'GET IN THE CAR!' he says.

And THAT is how I end up RIDING in the police car (which I LOVE).

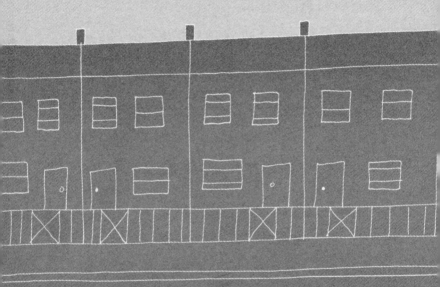

I am a detective. I use this as a chance to test my theories.

'The first suspects,' I tell Mr Maysmith, 'MUST be people who were in that kitchen.'

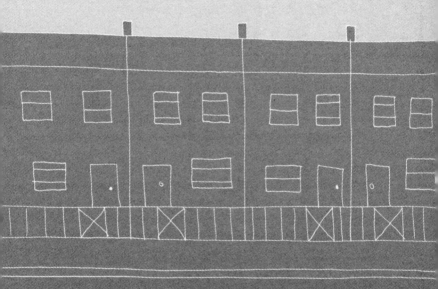

'Who were the *alibis* of the people in that kitchen?' I say.

Maysmith says nothing.

'Corner Boy's alibi,' I tell him, 'is his poo. They won't allow THAT in court!'

'ENOUGH!'

shouts Maysmith.

By now we've reached my house.
Suddenly I get *the fear*. (My mum
HATES me being a detective.)

'What will you say if my mum's here?' I
ask.

'I'll say you were at the school,' he
answers. 'We apprehended you for your
own safety.'

'Would you say I was at the *back* of the
school?' I ask. 'Looking for my ball?'

By now he's already knocked.

My mum answers. She looks at Maysmith.

'We found Rory at the back of the school,' he says. (*Fair play to him!*)

'I was looking for my ball,' I say.

'He was looking for his ball,' Maysmith confirms.

Mum looks at me. She doesn't care if I was looking for a *pot of gold*. She gives me the sort of look a witch gives, just before she eats you.

'You,' she hisses. 'IN.'

CHAPTER EIGHT:
Nerves

As I go up to my room, I am *tense*. For
the first time, I am thinking: *There was a
real-life KILLER at the school today, and I am
TERRIFIED*. But right now, I'm a lot more
scared of my mum.

But it is one of those times when you don't know how *annoyed* your mum will be, because you don't know what she KNOWS.

Is she coming up?

I can't tell. But for now, I tidy my room.
That only takes ten seconds. I just shove
everything under the bed.

I listen again.

Is she coming?

I figure: *If she does, I better be doing
something good. I should do homework! But I
don't have homework! I should find some!*

I nip next door and get her iPad. I go on a very *stupid* app called Mr Bolton's Grammar Zone, where you play annoying games about grammar.

I play one called *Splat the Verb*. There's a picture of Mr Bolton. Words come out of his mouth – first NOUNS (*egg, dog)* then ADJECTIVES (*big, small)* then VERBS (*hit, sing)*. You have to SPLAT the verbs.

I splat about two hundred. But I don't do what I WANT to do, which is to . . .

Splat Mr Bolton in the FACE with a wet SOCK filled with MANURE! **Kersplat.**

My mum STILL hasn't come. I'm thinking: *I'm not going to stay here being tortured in the Grammar Zone.*

I'll go outside.

'I BOUGHT you that *trampoline*!' my mum is *always* saying. 'And I NEVER see you use it!'

I figure: *She will now.*

I go outside to the trampoline. I start
bouncing. But I might still be in trouble,
so when Mum sees me, I figure I shouldn't
be too *playful*.

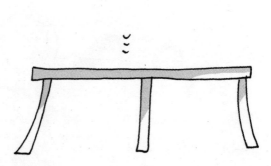

So I just do *the Sentry*. I bounce with my
arms by my side.

FINALLY Mum appears, but she STILL
doesn't even look . . .

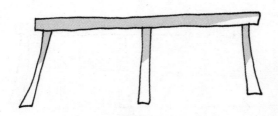

. . . Even though I am now bouncing
three metres high, looking very SERIOUS,
as if I'm the *fiercest SENTRY of all.*

She *still* doesn't look. I'm actually *annoyed* now.

So I mess about.

I do the Superman.

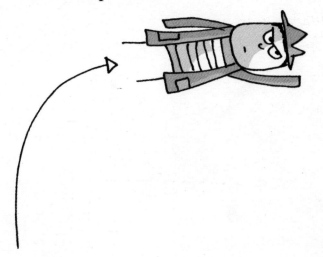

I do the Swan.

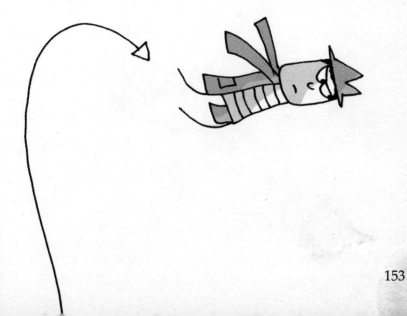

I do the Beetle on His Back.

I do the Worm.

I do the Forward Somersault.

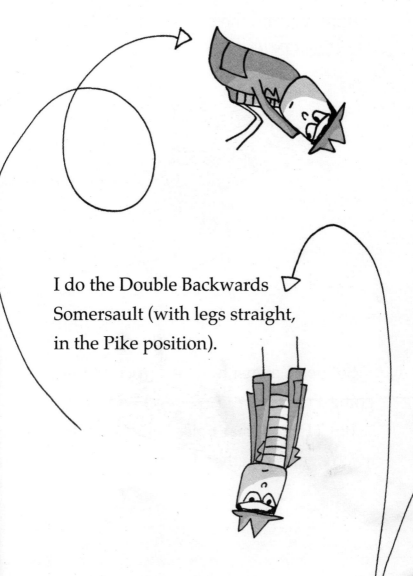

I do the Double Backwards
Somersault (with legs straight,
in the Pike position).

I then land with my foot between the trampoline and the metal and I *WHACK MYSELF ON THE BEJANGLES.*

So then I'm just hunched up, and I'm going *Errrrrrrrrr like a badger being sick.*

But THEN I hear noise behind me. I *quickly* get it together. I turn.

I see Cassidy's freckly face looming
over the fence.

'You OK?' she says.

'I'm *grand*!' I tell her. 'I didn't find out
about the roof, but I *did* find out that a bin
was moved and there was *smashed glass*
next to it.'

She says nothing.

'Are you OK?' I ask her.

'Never *better*,' she replies. 'Only I'm
thinking *I took the wrong hat*!'

'Someone has DIED,' I tell her. 'And you're thinking about HATS?!'

'I am!' she says. 'I want to go back to school to get another!'

'Cat,' I say, 'I just *went* to the school. I was taken home by the police.'

'Where were the police?' she says.

'They were all round the front of the school! There were LOADS of them!'

'So,' she says, 'we have to go in the back.'

I'm thinking: *I don't like how she said 'we'.*
At the same time, I like it too.

'I thought you couldn't be a detective
any more,' I say.

'And I won't be,' she replies. 'I'm just getting a hat – *in some style*. And if my dad finds out what we've done, that's my story. But when we're there, we can check if that flat roof overlooks the yard.'

At this, she winks. I suddenly realise she IS still being a detective after all. I am so happy I could SING (but that wouldn't be professional).

'Your mum's in the kitchen,'
she says. 'I suggest we climb
out through my garden!'
   I say nothing. I just follow.

Sometimes I think: *Maybe Cat is a brilliant genius who can make you do whatever she wants*. Five minutes after she arrived in my garden, we're reaching the dark alley that leads to the back of the school.

CRIME SCENE - DO NOT CROSS

CHAPTER NINE:
Into The Unknown

Silently, Cat leads me down that back alley.

At the end, we peek.

We're looking over an open field. We can see a lawnmower on the grass. We can see the old gym trampoline that's been pushed over by the classrooms. We can't see any police.

Cat smiles at me. (I swear . . . she's like this. When she's getting into danger, she smiles.)

'I'll race you,' she says.

She suddenly SPRINTS off.

Now, I am the third fastest runner in my class. I go after her like a *bullet*.

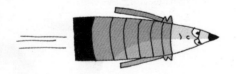

But it's like she turns into a *missile*, and she BLASTS off quicker still. I'm watching after her, amazed.

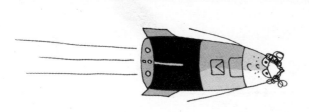

And that's how I hit the lawnmower.

BANG!

I pretend it's deliberate.
I soar up into the air.

I land with a somersault.

I then ROLL over to Cat, who is
crouching behind a yellow bin marked
SALT.

We both peek round the salt.

From here, we can see through the glass back door of the school. If any policemen appear, they'll see us.

'I'll go in first,' I whisper.

Crouching low, I sprint towards the door.

As I pass it, I LEAP across the concrete path, and I look up the corridor. I see nothing.

Kneeling, I crouch to the right of it. I land in a somersault (as if I was expecting *gunfire*). I look back at Cat.

Meanwhile, she just . . .
Strolls over to the door. She pushes it
open.

I am actually *annoyed*, because I am
being very *careful* and *professional*, but she
is being totally CASUAL.

I follow her. I find her in the lobby. She's staring at a cardboard cut-out of Mary Seacole, the famous nurse from Victorian times.

'I thought we were going to check that roof,' I tell her.

'Indeed,' she says. 'And to find me a new hat!'

She lopes off up the stairs.

I can't believe it. I always find that schools are very CREEPY places anyway when they're empty and the lights are off. You feel there could be GHOSTS. But now there could be POLICE. There could even be A KILLER.

But she's totally cool.

At the top, she pushes open the door to the corridor. There's a waxwork of a Viking outside the History Room. He looks freakily READY to come to life.

Cat doesn't care.

She strolls past the Science Lab. I happen to know that room has a glass tank full of *newts*. Just THINKING about *newts* makes me feel COLD inside.

But Cat's happy.

She strolls through to the big staircase.
It's like a swirling hole down to hell.

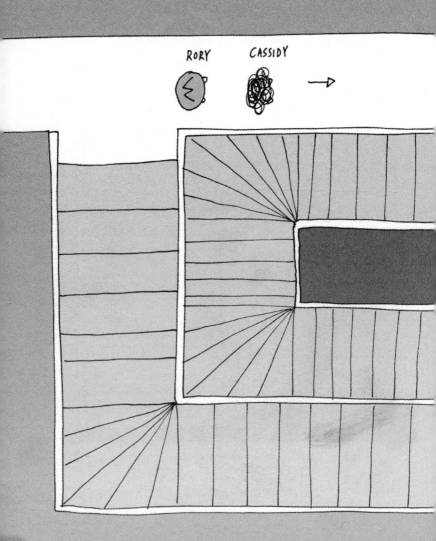

She's not bothered. I actually *want* her
to be scared now.

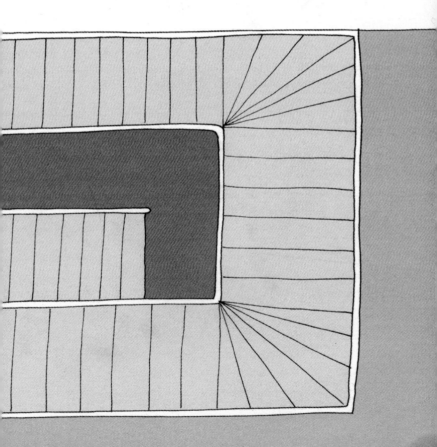

She pushes open the door to the Drama Studio. Now that's a WEIRD place at the best of times. There's a doorway that leads nowhere. There's a bowl filled with weapons and masks. I put one on.

So that's why when she turns – wearing a new hat – I'm *wearing the face of an ORC and holding a KNIFE.*

Yes, the knife is RUBBER. But she doesn't know. She SCREAMS.

I take the mask off.

Straight away, she's calm again.

'Why did you DO that?' she asks.

'You were being so CASUAL!'

'That was very stupid. You could have just given our position away to the police!'

'We need to get out of here!' she says.

We head for the door.

'But we need to check that roof,' I say, stopping her. '*Was* that the door you closed?'

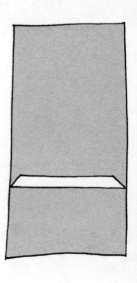

'Yes!' she says.

'And we don't *know* yet if it's over the back yard?'

'No!' she says.

'So will we look?' I say.

But I suddenly have a VERY BAD FEELING.

'The most evil criminal could be on the other side of that door!' I say.

'Well, if they are,' says Cat, 'they're very STUPID – to have done the crime, and then STAYED.'

'Let's just open that door,' she suggests, 'for one second!'

I look at her. I look at the door. It's one of those fire escape ones that you open with a bar.

We both put our hands on that bar.

I look into her eyes.

'One, two, three,' she mouths.

Then . . .

CRIME SCENE - DO NOT CROSS

CHAPTER TEN:
Above the Scene of the Crime

We push open that door.

We can see it's getting dark. We cannot see a criminal. We can see a flat roof. We cannot see if it's over the yard.

'How do we know if it's over the yard?' I whisper.

'Only one way to find out,' says Cat.

She strolls out. She peers down over the edge.

'What can you see?' I ask.

She doesn't tell me anything.

(*No one ever does!*)

I have to go to the edge myself, but I am SO *scared* of heights that I wriggle over like a big worm. I look down.

We *are* over that yard. I can see it all.

'But how would a killer have got down?' I ask.

'Like this,' she says.

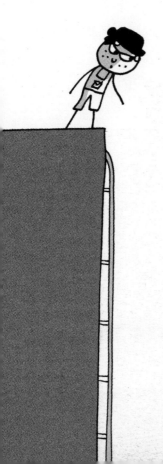

And she starts climbing down the drainpipe.

'How do we know that's strong enough to take your weight?' I ask.

'We know it was strong enough to take the killer's!' she says.

This is HORRIBLE.

Then it gets worse . . .

Stephen Maysmith appears in the yard below. Luckily, he doesn't see Cassidy. He's just ambling around like a big cow who's looking for some grass.

I wave to Cat. I point. She looks down. She gives me a look as if to say: *Oops*. She climbs back up.

Two seconds later, she's back on the
roof. She's moving towards the open door.
We're heading for safety.

'Oh my God,' I whisper. 'I am actually
SO scared of heights!'

'Me too!' says Cat.

'Me three!' says a voice.

And someone appears on the Science-lab roof.

My heart is about to leap from my mouth.

'Mr Meeton!' I say. 'Why are you here?'

'I just came out,' he says, 'to take a picture for *SuperMeet*! But then the door was shut and I got trapped!'

I can't believe it! It must have been HIM who did the crime!

'MOVE!' says Cat. She pulls me over.

We both SPRING to the door and pull it SHUT.

'LET ME IN!' Mr Meeton bellows, HAMMERING on the door.

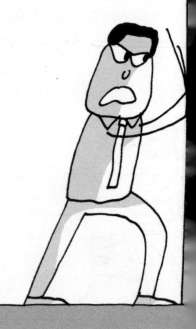

'I'd say he's giving away his position—'
Cat says.

'—to the police!' I finish.

'And I'd say it'd be better if they find
him. But not us.'

'LET ME IN!'

Mr Meeton shouts again, still beating on the door.

'I'd say even Stephen Maysmith heard that!' says Cat.

'So what do we do now?'

'We GO.'

And we do not hang about.

Ten seconds later, we are SPRINTING down the swirling staircase into hell.

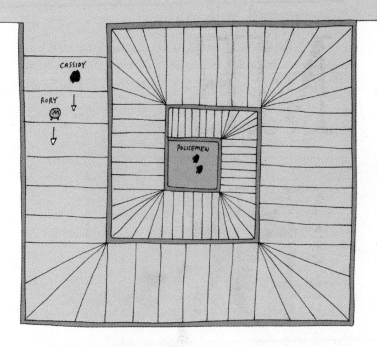

But the police appear at the bottom.

'Anyone up there?' they call.

We're not falling for that. We don't answer.

We just dodge back up the stairs,
then through the door to the third-floor
corridor.

'We should hide,' says Cat.

She takes my hand and pulls me into
the Science Lab.

'But where?' she says.

I look round. The only place I can see
is the big tank of newts. *I'm not going in
there!*

'Down,' I say.

I pull her under the workbench. There's a big gas bottle down there that they use for filling the Bunsen burners.

I look at Cat. She's still holding my hand. She squeezes it. I look in her eyes. She looks in mine. Then she turns.

'That window's open,' she says. 'If Mr Meeton is clever, he'll realise he can climb in.'

'We should shut it,' I say.
'We definitely should,' she replies.

The door opens.

'Is there someone here?' says a policeman.

We can see his shoes on the floor.

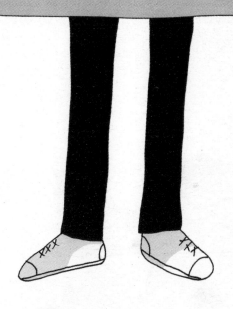

Staring into Cat's eyes, I don't even breathe. *Will he see us?*

As he leaves, and as he shuts the door, we both breathe out.

'He's going back to the Drama Studio,' whispers Cat.

'What now?' I whisper.

'We SHIFT.'

She counts them out: 'Three, two, one ...'

Then we SHIFT.

EMERGENCY EXIT →

CHAPTER ELEVEN:
We Shift

Two seconds later, we are out of the lab.

Eight seconds later, we're shooting past the Viking.

Thirty seconds later, we are PELTING down the back stairs.

I take the last flight with a LEAP.

As I land, a BIG THOUGHT hits me like a bomb.

'We didn't shut that window!'

I tell Cat.

She says nothing.

Then someone appears through the door.

It's Mr Bolton.

Cat darts behind Mary Seacole. He doesn't see her.

He does see *me*.

'Rory Branagan,' he says, 'the school is closed. The POLICE have just been here.'

'Did they find Mr Meeton?' I ask.

'What?' he says.

'He's on the roof. But there's a window open in the Science Lab. If he finds it, he might climb through and ESCAPE.'

Mr Bolton's face goes very still. 'Show me that window,' he says.

And as I lead him up the stairs I catch Cat's eye and mouth the word 'HELP!'

Thirty seconds later, Mr Bolton and I push open the door to the Science Lab.

Just then, a skinny foot appears.

Almost every cell in my body is telling me: *Get out, get out, get out NOW.* But the part that is a detective wants to SEE what will happen.

I stay.

I turn to Mr Bolton.

'We could try talking to him,' I suggest.

Mr Bolton braces himself like a COBRA.

Five seconds later, Mr Meeton comes
tumbling through the window. He jumps
down from the workbench.

'Good evening,' says Mr Bolton.

Mr Meeton is just a silhouette, so I can't
see his face, but I can tell . . .

He has just climbed down off the roof to find Mr Bolton standing in the dark like a weird goblin saying, 'Good evening'.

I'd say he's surprised. But he keeps cool.

'Good evening, Mr Bolton,' he answers. '*It's* a surprise to see you . . . And of course I would spell it *ITS I, T, no apostrophe, S.*'

'Er, no,' Mr Bolton corrects him. 'Because in this case, IT'S is short for IT IS, so there *is* an apostrophe, because—'
But Mr Bolton doesn't get to finish.

Mr Meeton *lamps* him with the stool.

BANG.

Bolton is down.

Now there's just me, blocking the way.

I am on the verge of a heart attack, but I keep my voice steady.

'Mr Meeton,' I say, 'you've been my favourite teacher since Year One.'

'Thank you,' he says.

'But I cannot let you pass.'

He is now like a snake about to bite.
'Why?' he asks.

And my heart is beating **SO**
loud as I say it: 'Because you killed
Ms Rhodes.'

'Why would I want to do a thing like
that?' he says quietly.

'Maybe you didn't *want* to,' I answer. 'Maybe you just came up here to clear your head. You took a selfie. You pretended you were a cool guitar hero. But inside you *knew* you'd just been *embarrassed* in a school talent show by the Toad. And you looked down, you saw her and you wanted to KILL her!'

'I did NOT want to kill her!' he answers.

'But you went down there and you DID it!'

'I did NOT!' he says.

And then I think of the GLASS, and I work it out.

'So then you THREW something at her!' I say.

'What would I have thrown?'

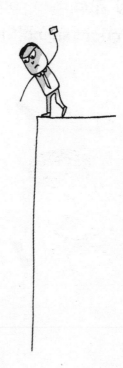

'The thing in your hand,' I answer.
'Your PHONE!'

He says nothing. But I can SEE I'm right.

'You hit her so hard, she went DOWN,' I say. 'And then you *panicked*. You realised you might spend the rest of your life in

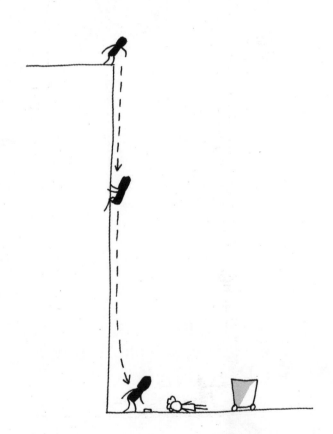

prison. So you climbed down. You got your phone. Then you couldn't get up, so you pushed over the bin, and you climbed the drainpipe!'

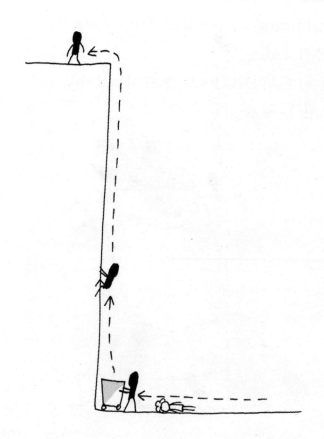

Mr Meeton doesn't admit to *any* of this. He just says, 'Rory, why are you doing this?'

'Because,' I tell him, 'I am becoming a detective!'

'You'll have a job doing *that*,' he spits, 'considering your whole family are CRIMINALS!'

'You CANNOT say that about my mum!' I shout.

'I'll say it about your dad then!'

'Before he had me, my dad was a *two-time World Rally Driving champion*,' I tell him.

'So it must have been *after* he had you,' he sneers, 'that he became a CRIMINAL!'

'What?!!!' I say.

I am now very, very ANGRY with Mr Meeton. But I want him to keep talking. I *need* that.

So it's a bad moment for Cat to help.

Mr Meeton and I hear her at the same time. We turn. We see a tall, dark figure through the window above the Science-lab door.

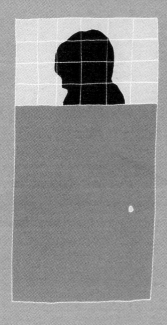

'WHAT is that?' says Mr Meeton.

He doesn't know *what the HECK* is out there.

But I do.

It's Cat, holding up Mary Seacole.

Well, I *think* it's that.

But, in fact, Mr Meeton opens the door,
and he grabs in . . .

Corner Boy, dressed as a Viking.

He has the axe, he has the helmet, but he doesn't use them. He just stumbles in and *smacks* the workbench.

Still, he's distracted Mr Meeton. And THAT's what starts the *action* . . .

CHAPTER TWELVE:
Action. Fast, Lethal Action

Cat makes her entrance.
And it's a good one.

She SLAMS open the door. She
SPRINTS forward, roaring, using *Mary
Seacole as a spear*.

Mr Meeton blocks her with the stool.
She falls.

I grab Seacole.

I THWAP Mr Meeton in the face.

He doesn't go down. But *he stumbles
into Corner Boy,* and unfortunately he . . .

. . . touches Corner Boy's glasses.

Corner Boy ***EXPLODES***. He kicks, *punches*. Then he gets Mr Meeton in a headlock and he *drives* him into the newts.

SMASH.

The newts *panic*. One of them tries to hide up Mr Meeton's nose.

'Quick, Corner Boy,' I say, 'get up on that workbench.'

He does.

'Open the window,' I say.

He does.

'Now JUMP.'

He does.

Mr Meeton can't believe it.

'What are you doing?' he says. 'You're killing your friends!'

'*I told you, I am a DETECTIVE,*' I say. 'And I have *noticed* something under that window.'

'What is it?' he says.

'It's a TRAMPOLINE!!' I tell him.

Just then Corner Boy *hits* that trampoline. We can all see him as he shoots back *up* by the window. He's going 'GERONIMO!' and he's waving his arms like a mad duck.

'Cat,' I tell her, 'go.'

'I don't want to leave you!'

'YOU MUST!' I tell her. For one second, she just looks at me.

Then . . .

she goes.

I jump up.

I look at Mr Meeton. He's pulling a newt from his hair.

'You are such a LOSER!' I tell him.

'I have had ENOUGH of you!' he says.

And as he comes for me, I swear he'd KILL me if he could.

But he can't. Because I jump.

And that's when I get *really* scared. I am SO scared of heights, and the trampoline seems so, so, so, so far off in the darkness.

For a moment, I shut my eyes. I feel like I'm LEAPING down to *certain death*.

But one moment later . . .

I HIT the trampoline and I BOUNCE HIGHER THAN I'VE EVER *BOUNCED* BEFORE! I have time to do the Superman . . .

The Chicken . . .

And the Worm.

Then I bounce down. I do the DOUBLE BACKWARDS SOMERSAULT (with legs in the Pike position).

I land PERFECTLY!

As I land, I find Cat and
Corner Boy waiting.

'Let's go!' Cat says.

We all just sprint off
round the corner.

And THAT is when
we bump into a HUGE,
DARK FIGURE . . .

CHAPTER THIRTEEN:
A Huge, Dark Figure

It's actually Stephen Maysmith.

I get him right in the stomach. (Luckily he's well padded!)

'GO STRAIGHT HOME,' he shouts.
'A SUSPECTED CRIMINAL is at
large!'

'Mr Meeton?' I say. 'He's through that
door. Third floor up, second door on the
left.'

'Er, correction,' says Corner Boy. 'He's
just jumped out the window.'

'RIGHT!' bellows Stephen Maysmith.
He charges over like a hippo.

By then Mr Meeton is hitting the
trampoline. He bounces up *well*.

He lands. And that's when Stephen
Maysmith PUNCHES his lights out and
whips on the handcuffs.

It is *quite* a punch. I swear . . .

When Mr Meeton comes round, he will have one *heck* of a sore head, and he'll be tied to a trampoline.

I turn to my friends.

'Corner Boy, I could NOT believe it when *you* turned up *dressed as a Viking*!'

'I *told* you I would help solve this case,' he says, 'and I did!'

'You definitely did!' I tell him. 'From this day forward, I will call you . . . Detective POO!'

I just say that for a joke. But then for a moment I'm worried Corner Boy might be *offended*. But then I see he's *shaking* with laughter.

'Just messing!' I tell him. 'From this day on, we will call you . . .'

'Hang on,' says Cat. 'Corner Boy, what would you *like* us to call you?'

Corner Boy likes this question. He
thinks about it.

'I would like to be called,' he says,
' . . . Special Agent Corner Boy!'
'And you *shall*!' says Cat.
He looks so pleased. But then . . .
'Still,' he says, 'my mum thinks I'm in
my room, cleaning out my guinea pigs.
I better get back before she SUSPECTS
something, so I can't stand here talking to
you *two LOSERS*!'

Then *suddenly* he SPRINTS off across the field.

I turn to Cat.

'That was *quite* an adventure!' I say.

'It was!' she agrees. 'But what do you say we keep it all to ourselves?'

'Hey,' I tell her, 'if we bring down bad guys, we don't do it because we're losers like Mr Meeton, who won't do anything unless one hundred people hear of it. We do it because *bad guys need bringing DOWN!*'

255

'*Deadly Branagan,*' she says, 'you're the best!'

I am about to say something back like: 'Cat Callaghan, YOU'RE the best!'

But she turns and walks off.

And for a second I am actually very sad she's walked off. I am also very sad for Ms Rhodes. I am also very shocked my dad is a criminal. I am also very bothered I can't talk about this to anyone

But just then Cat stops. She smiles.

Even so, I think, I am still very glad I'm here.

And I look at Cat.

I look round. I see trees. I see stars.
I say nothing.

CRIME SCENE - DO NOT CROSS

CHAPTER FOURTEEN:
An Epic Ending

The school is closed the next day while the police complete their *investigation*.

They do find out one very *important* thing, which they announce on the news. I miss it, but Cat comes round and tells me.

'Ms Rhodes is not dead,' she says.

I'm stunned by that.

'But . . .' I say. 'Why did everyone think she was?'

'Because you ANNOUNCED it in the playground!' says Cat. 'I said your big mouth would get you into *trouble*.'

This is VERY EMBARRASSING, I'm
thinking. *Will Ms Rhodes be ANNOYED*
when she hears I *told everyone she'd* died?

But it's not the first thing on her mind
when she comes round . . .

A day later, the Toad wakes up in hospital. Her first words, apparently, are:

'I smell PUDDING!'

But then her eyes close again.

The next day, the school reopens, and Mrs Winscombe – of all people – makes a speech.

'I am happy to announce that Ms Rhodes *is* recovering,' she says. 'But *she will be retiring*. I was very proud to have served her dinners for thirty-eight years. She fed a lot of children in that time. Her peach crumbles, in particular, were *delicious*, and I shall miss them.'

Suddenly everyone cries.

Two weeks later, we have the final of St Bart's Got Talent. Ms Rhodes comes out of retirement to be the host.

'Mr Meeton was going to host,' she says, 'but he's now in PRISON.'

That gets a massive cheer.

Cat is in the final. She takes the stage by leaping *backwards* off the top of the gym ladder! People can't *believe* it.

At the end, everyone is cheering, '*The Cat, the Cat, the Cat.*'

But her cheers are totally drowned out
by those when the Toad announces that
*'Next up, with his Famous "Grammar Rap",
will be . . . Misterrrrr BOLTON!'*

Even before he comes on, EVERYONE
is chanting: *'Big Bad Bolton Man . . .
I say YOU, my Bolton Man! (Oh
yeah!)'* which is the rap I made up when
I solved The Big Cash Robbery.

As Mr Bolton comes on, he is strutting like a *penguin* to the beat. '*Big Bad Bolton Man . . . I say YOU, my Bolton Man! (Oh yeah!)*'

The thing is . . .

When Mr Bolton rapped before,
Mr Meeton filmed it and put it on the
internet, thinking Mr Bolton was a *joke*.
But Mr Bolton's 'Grammar Rap' has
become a HUGE HIT. *It has been shared two
hundred thousand times*. So as the Bolton
Man hits the chorus now, we *definitely*
know the words.

Mr Bolton holds out the mic as we all go . . .

'IT'S is short for IT IS.

ITS means BELONGING TO IT.

WHO'S is short for WHO IS.

WHOSE means BELONGING TO **WHO**!!'

'These are the rules of apostrophes, If you forget them *KISS MY SHOE!'* We all roar the last bit *so loud…*

. . . aliens, far off in space, would probably hear, and they'd think there was a BIG BAD BOLTON MAN telling them to 'kiss my shoe'.

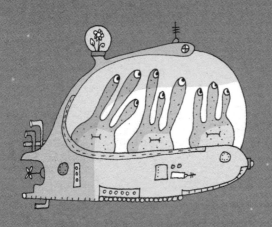

And I think of that. I think we just
solved another crime. And I smile.

The End

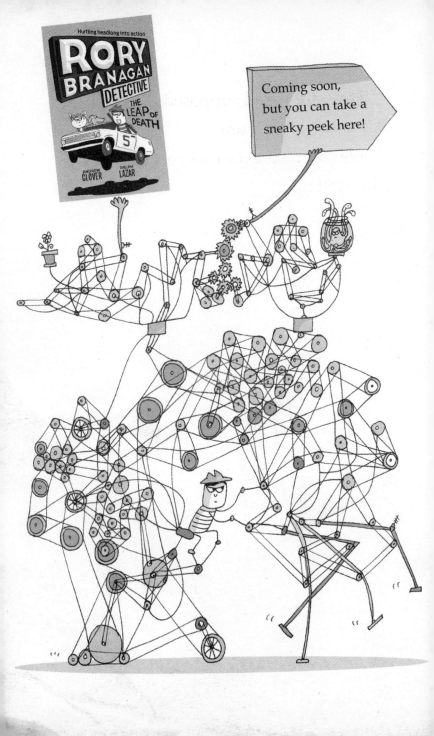

'How are we all supposed to get to Car Bonanza?' says Mum.

'We could take the campervan!' says Mrs Welkin.

I didn't even know Mrs Welkin was here. It turns out she is, and she has a camper van.

It is a big old thing with beds and a kitchen for making hot chocolate. It is *BRILLIANT*, but it sure is slow!

As we go to Car Bonanza, we get a line of cars behind us.

'Mrs Welkin,' I say, 'we're making a traffic jam!'

'I don't call this a traffic jam,' she says. 'I call it a parade!'

Just then, we come over the hill and see Car Bonanza. It looks EPIC.

I see the World's Highest Ever Jump
(done without parachute). There's a plane
ready to lift the jumper into the sky so
they can LEAP out into a big net. (Just
thinking of that makes me sick!)

We park by The Leap of Death.

'Our car will drive down this hill,' announces a woman with a mic. 'It will hit 100 kilometres per hour. It will speed to the ramp, then jump this tank which contains ONE HUNDRED HUNGRY CROCODILES!!'

I'm thinking: *What NUTTERS would do that?* (Little do I know, those NUTTERS will be US!)

To be continued . . .